LITTLE EGRET and TORO

LITTLE EGRET
and
TORO

by **ROBERT VAVRA**

drawings by **JOHN FULTON**

Channel Photographics

Channel Photographics / Channel Kids
980 Lincoln Ave.Suite 200B,
San Rafael California, 94901
T: 415.456.2934 F: 415.456.4124

www.channelphotographics.com

Published by Adrianne Casey and Steven Goff

ISBN-13: 978-0-9819942-3-9

US/Canadian Distribution -
Publishers Group West
1700 Fourth Street,
Berkeley, CA 94710
T: 877.528.1444

© – Robert Vavra
© – John Fulton

First published by William Collins Sons Co. Ltd London 1966

Printed and bound in China by Global PSD,
www.globalpsd.com

Channel Photographics & Global Printing, Sourcing & Development (Global PSD), in association with American Forests and the Global ReLeaf programs, will plant two trees for each tree used in the manufacturing of this book. Global ReLeaf is an international campaign by American Forests, the nation's oldest nonprofit conservation organization and a world leader in planting trees for environmental restoration.

For Weems and the Sparrow

Many years ago, near a great marsh in Southern Spain, lived a baby fighting bull who was not afraid of anything. His fur was black and shiny. And his eyes were dark and soft, except when he was angry and then they glittered like hot coals.

And although this baby bull's horns were only small bumps on his head, he was always ready to charge. But after all, are not Spanish bulls the bravest bulls in the world?

Not far from where the baby bull lived was the nest of a cattle egret. Cattle egrets always have serious expressions on their faces. In fact, the angrier they look, the happier they are. The favourite food of these white birds is the small, unpleasant ticks that cling to the big, black bulls.

One day when the mother egret left her nest, a young fox sneaked up to the baby egret. But just as he pounced on the nest the baby bull appeared.

"You should be ashamed of yourself," bellowed the baby bull to the fox.

But the fox only showed his fangs and snarled.

So the little bull lowered his head, charged and chased the fox away.

Then he returned to the nest.

"I can never thank you enough," said the baby egret.

The little bull smiled and replied, "When you are big and can fly, and your beak is sharp, then you can pick ticks from my back. And since you are a cattle egret, I shall simply call you Little Egret, for that is your name."

"And I shall call you Toro," said Little Egret, "because Toro means bull in Spanish."

And from that day, the bull and the bird became the best of friends.

Time passed, and **Little Egret's** white feathers grew longer, and soon he could sail through the sky like an arrow.

Toro, the bull, became big and strong and his horns were sharp and curved as a crescent moon.

When it rained hard and for many days, as it often does in Southern Spain, Little Egret would shelter himself between Toro's great legs.

And when the scorching sun beat down in the summer, as it often does in Southern Spain, Little Egret would return from the pond to fan and cool Toro.

Every morning Little Egret, who liked an early breakfast, would waken his friend. Then, even though Toro would have liked to sleep longer, he would turn his head to one side so that Little Egret could pick all the fat-bodied ticks from his great neck.

Later, Toro would graze in the pasture, and as he walked through the grass his large hoofs would stir up grasshoppers and other insects for Little Egret's lunch.

Although Toro had never been out of his pasture, it seemed to him that he had seen the whole world. For you see, in the quiet evening Little Egret would tell him where he had been and what he had seen during the day.

Of the blue ocean and the boats that floated on it.

Of the great rock of Gibraltar which was even larger than Toro.

And even of the strange, hump-backed camels not far away in North Africa.

Toro liked to play at fighting with the other bulls.
Back and forth they would push each other.
Little Egret would try to help. But Toro always won.
He was the biggest, strongest bull in the pasture.

When he and Little Egret walked together, all the other bulls turned to admire them.

One day, men on horses came into the field to choose the bravest bulls for the bullfights. When they tested Toro by chasing him and prodding him with their long poles, Little Egret shot from the sky to peck at their heads and knock their hats to the ground.

But the men soon saw that Toro was the bravest bull in the pasture—the most ferocious bull in Spain!

One afternoon, not much later, Little Egret returned from a long flight to find Toro proudly rubbing his horns against a dead tree.

Toro was so excited.

"The men were here today to pick a bull for next Sunday's fight in Sevilla," he shouted, "and they chose me as the bravest of all!"

"But Toro, you will never come back," cried Little Egret. "Bulls never return from the ring and from the matador's sword."

"Don't worry, little friend," said Toro. "I will be the bravest bull that they have ever seen in Sevilla. No one will stick me with a sword."

Poor Little Egret's heart sank and tears came to his small yellow eyes, for he knew that this was not true. Although he had never told Toro, one Sunday afternoon he had flown to Sevilla where he had watched the bullfight from which no bull returns.

But no matter how hard he tried, Little Egret could not convince Toro that all bulls who went to the bullfight ended up in the butcher's shop. Finally he lost his patience and stamped off shrieking, "Oh, how can you be so bull-headed!"

Then that fateful day arrived and the men came and put Toro into a big box.

As Little Egret followed the truck that carried Toro to Sevilla, he was so sad he thought his heart would break.

When they arrived in Sevilla, the bullring was packed with people.

The band played the most brilliant music.

And the ladies wore their best black lace mantillas.

Finally the old president of the bullring signalled for the trumpets to be sounded, and the bullfighters strutted proudly across the golden sand.

Then the great wooden door was opened and Toro charged into the ring.

Little Egret, who could not bear to watch the fight, sat behind the ring sobbing his heart out.

"Oh, what can I do?" he wondered, as he paced back and forth on the wall of the corral.

A wise old ox who happened to be in the corral, heard the bird's sobs and asked, "Why are you so sad, my white-feathered friend?"

And then Little Egret told the ox about Toro.

"My, oh my," said the old ox. "That is indeed sad. But you say that your friend is the bravest bull in Spain? Well, then, there is one chance. But the people of Sevilla no longer remember how to pardon the life of a brave bull. Only the old, short-sighted president remembers."

"But how, oh how?" pleaded Little Egret. "Please hurry, Toro is already in the ring!"

"Well," said the ox, "when I was a calf, if a bull was very brave all the people took out their white handkerchiefs and waved them above their heads. Then the president ordered the bull to be sent back to his pasture to live peacefully for the rest of his life."

"You say the old president has poor eyesight?" said Little Egret, who thought for a moment, then shot into the air like a white arrow.

As Little Egret flew over the bullring, he saw Toro charging like a locomotive at the matador's cape.

He sailed high over the city and across the river towards
the marshes.

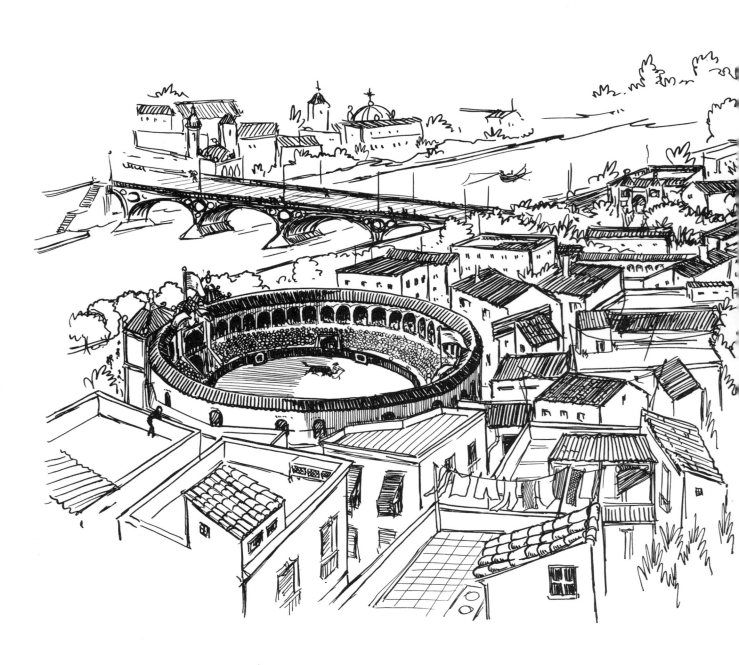

Hundreds of other cattle egrets were peacefully feeding or sunning themselves when Little Egret, screeching the egret cry for help, flew down to them.

Hearing the cries, the great flock of birds rose like a white cloud and followed Little Egret towards Sevilla.

Back at the bullring, the frightened matador was just drawing his sharp sword.

"This is the bravest bull I have ever seen," said the old president.

And just as the matador was aiming his sword at Toro, who now realised that Little Egret had told him the truth,

the white cloud of cattle egrets

dropped down and circled round the ring.

From his seat, the old, short-sighted president saw the birds across the ring and shouted, "Sound the trumpets! I knew it! I knew it! The people of Sevilla still remember how to save the life of a brave bull! Look at all those white handkerchiefs!"

And all round the ring, other old people, like the short-sighted president, mistook the birds for white handkerchiefs.

"Save the bull!" they shouted and began waving their own handkerchiefs until the whole ring was a sea of white.

The trumpets blasted the most glorious salute.

The band played even more brilliantly than before.

The crowd applauded until the bullring began to shake.

And the great wooden door swung open and Toro proudly left the ring and walked slowly back to the corral.

Then Little Egret gave a shout of thanks to his friends who flew back to the marsh.

Behind the ring, he found Toro who cried, "Oh, Little Egret, you were right, and if it hadn't been for you and your friends, I would now be hanging in some butcher's shop."

"Just rest," said Little Egret happily as he picked a fat tick from Toro's shoulder.

The next day, Toro was taken back to his pasture where Little Egret was waiting for him.

How happy they were.

And even today, though many years have passed, the

people of Sevilla still remember and talk about that afternoon of the "white handkerchiefs" and about Toro, the bravest of bulls.